a story about a young girl with a BIG imagination

A JOURNEY OF
REFLECTION

WHO DO YOU SEE WHEN YOU LOOK IN THE MIRROR?

MAVIS
SYBIL

CONTENTS

STORM CLOUDS

"Gina, are you ready? We need to go. Now!" Mama yelled.

"Just give me one more minute!" The room was darkening as big, heavy clouds covered the sky. We'd lived in Florida our whole lives, and we'd lived through thunderstorms from the hurricanes before. But this one was different.

I shoved the last of my favorite things into the duffel bag I'd been given - my dresses, books, crayons, a vintage Gameboy that my uncle James gave me for Christmas, and of course, Pebbles' toys. She was in her cat carrier and Mama had stuck her in the car already. This was all that was left.

The room got darker, and so I threw the bag over my shoulder and ran outside. The wind had already picked up, bending the tree in our yard so far I was sure it'd snap. I shut the door to the car hard. My hands were shaking as I tried to buckle myself in. Mama had already started the car and we peeled out of the driveway. I looked out the back window at our house getting smaller and smaller and smaller, until it wasn't there anymore.

"We're lucky we made it out when we did. Are you okay?" Mama asked once we reached the highway. We could finally breathe now that the dark clouds were sufficiently behind us.

I shrugged. "I'm okay." Mostly. "Can I hold Pebbles?"

"I don't know if we should let her out into the car. You can let her head out though. I'm sure she's just as frightened as the rest of us."

"Okay." I opened Pebble's carrier, just a little bit so she could stick her little face out. I wasn't sure if Mama was right about her being frightened though. Pebbles had been yelling at us all at the start of the ride, but once we got farther away from the storm, she calmed. It's like she knew we were safe.

"Mrreoow!" Pebbles trilled as she popped her head out of the carrier. She looked around and readjusted into a loaf. You know, the way that cats sit when all of their paws are under their body. Mama and I called it that because she looked like a loaf of bread. I pet her cheeks and she closed her eyes, happy to have the attention back on her.

Pebbles was my best friend. Like, of all time. Mama had found her when she was a tiny little kitten in the dumpster behind her work. She was part of a litter of four, Mama said. She was also the only one to make it. I was only five then, but Mama couldn't just let her sit in some shelter. She was too perfect for that. With her big honey eyes and long grey-blue fur, Pebbles was something special. We grew up together, Pebbles and I. She never left my side, except for when I had to go to school. Even then, she liked to walk me to the bus stop every morning, and she'd wait for me when I was coming back.

Everyone knew her too. I'd even asked Mama if I could start an Instagram for her since she was 35 years old in cat years. That qualified! Mama had laughed and said no. Apparently ten-year-olds can't have Instagram. Even if it is for their cat. And you know, that didn't make sense to me because Jaylen's mom said she could have an Instagram and she was also ten! Mama said it was different because Jaylen sometimes did commercials, and her mother ran the page. It wasn't fair, but Mama wouldn't say no to something unless she had a good reason for it.

I fell asleep watching the trees and towns in the distance flash by in a blur. By the time my eyes opened, we were somewhere new, cruising past large expanses of land, with cows and horses and lots of farmland.

"Where are we?" I yawned and rubbed the sleep from my eyes.

"Morning sleepy." I could see Mama smile in the rearview mirror. "We're in Georgia. Just halfway to James' place. Just a few more hours. How's Pebbles doing?"

"She's good. She ate all her food though."

"You can give her some water in the little cup." Mama handed me a thermos of water, the kind with a cup as its lid. "We'll stop for the night soon."

"Okay." I poured a little bit of water out and held it in front of Pebbles, watching her sniff and lap it up. "She's thirsty."

"I bet she is. You go ahead and drink some too. I promise it won't be much cooler up here than it is back home."

"Uncle James lives in Atlanta, right? That's like... a really big city. It sounds scary."

"It'll be fine, I promise. He's so excited to see you, you know. He called while you were sleeping. Apparently, he and his roommate made a whole desk area for you to do your drawings. Isn't that nice?"

"It is but isn't that an awful lot to do if we're just staying for a little bit?"

Silence hung in the air. A sigh escaped from between Mama's lips, and she glanced back at me, pulling to a stop at the red light.

"Well, honey, there's a chance we might not be back for a good while. We still don't really know how hard the storm hit."

A pressure began to form in my chest as I realized what she was saying. I took in a deep breath, until my lungs began to ache, then slowly let it out, the pressure leaving with the air.

"Will...will I be going to a new school?"

Mama nodded. "Probably. I wouldn't worry about it too much right now though, alright? It's summer so we've got time to figure things out."

I took one more deep breath. "Maybe I'll go to one of those art schools. They have those in Atlanta, right?"

"They most certainly do," Mama said. Maybe a little too fast, but it didn't matter. There was enough to keep my imagination busy until we stopped at a motel for the night. Pebbles slept by my face that night, and I wondered what she thought of all this. What if she couldn't go outside again like she used to? Was she scared too, like I was? Did she miss our home already like I did? The tears started to well up in my eyes, emotions catching up to me, and I put my face in the pillow to stifle them.

The next morning was bright. It nearly hurt my eyes, how much the sun shone. You could hear the bugs chirp - yes, the bugs - while we loaded ourselves back into the car. I strapped Pebbles' carrier back in and sat next to her. Her head poked out of the little space I'd left for her. Her forehead came out first, followed by her ears that popped upright.

"Pebbles, we're going to be in a new home today," I remarked with as much cheer as I could muster. She just looked at me, then at Mama, who had started the car. Pebbles' head went back into the carrier.

Mama insisted on listening to the radio when we drove. Sometimes it was good, and we'd catch something on NPR or a classic rock or country station. Sometimes it was less good, and we listened to the sound of the car's engine rumbling as it worked to propel us down the highway, this being preferable to screeching static.

We didn't talk too much either. Mama and I were both introverts. That's what the Meyer's Briggs test that Rachel had asked me to take said. We were kind of friends, Rachel and I. We had been really good friends up until 5th grade. When we started at middle school, we were sworn sisters. After that first year though, things really changed. Rachel changed. By the time Christmas came around, she had a boyfriend. She straightened her curly hair, stating it was just far too unruly to ever be considered attractive. She even snuck in makeup from her mother's purse to put on in the bathrooms before first period. She was popular.

And of course, she would be popular. She was so nice! But I didn't care about those things like she did. The boys were boring. And not everyone that was nice to her was going to be there for her like I had been. I knew things about her nobody else did. Like, I knew her favorite flavor of ice cream was cookies and cream, even though she told everyone it was chocolate. And I knew she secretly really liked to look up all the creepy fairy tale stories, even though her mom didn't let her read Harry Potter or any other magic books. I knew all of her secrets. And she knew all of mine.

That's what being friends was supposed to be about. But everything changed and it changed so slowly I hadn't even realized it until I was away from her, thinking about a new city and a new school and if there would be a new Rachel. There could never be another Rachel. I would simply be friendless, forever. I looked over at Pebbles. Friendless with humans. Forever.

After what felt like a whole year, we made it to Uncle James' home.

"GINA!" His voice boomed from across the parking garage. I swung my legs out of the open car door and waved at him, a grin breaking out across my face for the first time in a day.

"Hi Uncle James!" I yelled back at him. Mama handed me my duffel and a suitcase, and we began unloading the packed car. Uncle James sprinted to us and hugged my mom.

"Thank god y'all made it up here alright." He picked up the two biggest suitcases. "How was the drive? Not too much traffic?"

Mama groaned. "It's worse than Orlando, I swear, James. How do you get to work every day like this?"

"Early," Uncle James said with a laugh. I walked around to the other side of the car and took Pebbles out. She meowed in protest to the movement, settling only when we put her on top of the cart Uncle James had brought for the rest of our stuff.

"Pebbles has never been in a parking garage before," I observed aloud. "I mean, we shouldn't let her out. I was just saying. It's new for her."

Mama nodded. "It is, yes. There are a lot of new things for all of us."

Uncle James put a hand on my shoulder and squeezed it. "Oh hey, we should go to the park later. There's a dog park too next to it. Maybe Pebbles can come with us."

That made me laugh. "Pebbles can't go on walks with us! She's a cat. Cats don't wear leashes."

Uncle James shrugged. "I don't know, I've seen cats on leashes."

We all laughed at the thought and went inside. Uncle James lived in a condo. It was a lot smaller than our house had been, but it was a lot bigger than I thought it would be. There were three rooms. Mama and I got the room that had been a joint office for Uncle James and his roommate Ben. It was kind of good that we had less stuff now since we had to fit all of our things into one closet. She took the hanging spots. I got the drawers in the dresser. It was tight, but it'd do for now.

That night, Uncle James took us around to the park. It was huge, bigger than any park I'd ever been to. It wasn't like being by the ocean, but it was still nice. It was good to see something other than the grey we'd seen on our drive to the park itself.

"I don't think I'm a city girl," I mused as we walked around the park, popsicle in hand.

"How would you know?" Uncle James asked teasingly. "You've only been here for three hours!"

I shrugged. "It's so... grey. It's not alive like the beach is."

He and Mama both nodded. They had both grown up by the beaches in Florida. They knew what I meant. There may be more movement in the city, more cars, and people. But the ocean was alive. Everything was alive - even the water and the sand and the shells. You could feel it.

"It's not. But it's alive in different ways," Mama added, sensing what I had begun to observe. "You might be more city girl than you think."

"That's true. I miss home though."

We walked quietly after that. There was no easy way to talk about this. I knew that. You could have cut the tension like a knife. It wasn't any of our faults that the storms had gotten so bad. We didn't control the weather. But everything that I had ever known was probably gone. Everything Mama had known was probably gone. I just didn't get how she was so cool about it. Or, how she could pretend she was if she wasn't. The longer we walked, and the more time passed, the more the pressure in my chest built up again. I tried to breathe, like Mama had taught me to when I felt my feelings get so big.

The air smelled like freshly cut grass and sunscreen and rain. Golden rays shone down upon us, warming my skin. It was such a change from where we had just left. The image of the tree in our front yard flashed behind my eyes. It had been so grey back there. So cloudy and windy. Usually, it felt like this. Warm and glowing. Back home, the air smelled like sea salt. It smelled cleaner. I let the breath go, and the thoughts with it.

STARTING OVER

Pebbles had peed on the couch when we got back.

On the couch! Pebbles never went to the bathroom anywhere except her litter box. Ever.

Uncle James was so angry, I could tell. His face got all puffy and red, but he tried so hard to be nice. I helped him get together paper towels and cleaners, and Mama ran to the shop with Uncle James' roommate to buy the special enzyme cleaner to get the smell out.

"This was such a nice couch too," Uncle James grumbled under his breath. Everything was almost entirely clean, but the smell lingered.

"I'm sorry, she doesn't usually do this. Like, ever. She's so good." I helped tie off the garbage bag. Pebbles had been quarantined into our room after we had gotten back from the park and seen the mess.

Uncle James sighed. He sat down on the floor beside the couch and patted the spot beside him.

"I know she's a good cat," he said, putting his arm over my shoulder. "Just a change for us all, right? I guess there will be some bumps along the way."

"It's scary." The tears started to well up in my eyes, maybe for the first time since leaving home. Everything felt like it was crashing down all over again. "She probably just wants to go back home. I want to go back home."

Uncle James pulled me in and hugged me tight. It was all too much, and I finally cried, harder than I'd cried in a very long time. A week had passed since we had to pack up and leave our home back in Florida. It wasn't too bad, it really wasn't.

But everything was so different. Life here was so different. The elevator was so noisy. We had to drive to go to the park. There were no beaches nearby to run on or seashells to collect. Actually, collecting things was seen as weird here, and people gave me strange looks when I tried to collect rocks on the streets. The cars were loud, the buildings were so tall. There were so many people. Too many people. Everyone was always talking. It wasn't the same. It wasn't home.

I cried until I didn't have tears left to cry. Uncle James rubbed my back, very classically awkward in his attempts to be comforting.

"I'm sorry," I sniffled and wiped my nose with the back of my hand. Uncle James' shirt was now spotted with wet spots from my tears and snot. Now I felt worse because I ruined his shirt.

"Don't worry, bug." He waved his hand. "I know it's a really big change, and not one that you or your Mama chose. She'd have you back in your home in no time, believe me. It's an adjustment for all of us. I'm sure you're tired of hearing that, but it is what it is for right now. We'll get another litter box, okay? I googled that that could help. And we'll take it day by day, yeah?"

I nodded. "Do you think our house is still there? Or my school?"

"I haven't heard anything yet, but as soon as we do, I'll tell you. I know your Mama probably wants to tell you this herself, but I do think you might want to prepare to be here for a while. Even if your home's okay, not everyone's house is, and the news says there's loads of flooding still. It's just going to take some waiting out. But don't you worry. It's okay to be sad, you know. It's okay to feel like that. But you can't let it take over, alright? You got to move on. It's all any of us can do."

He patted my head and let go of me. I groaned and laid back on the rug. "Why did this have to happen to me? I hate it. I just want to go back home, I miss the beach and I miss my friends and I miss my bed and my room and everything."

"I wish I could say something to make it better." Uncle James shrugged. "Sometimes the cards just don't fall the way you think they will. You just make the best of it."

The front door opened, and Mama and Ben came in.

"We brought ice cream!" Mama said with a smile. It fell ever so slightly when she saw my puffy face. "Everything okay?"

I nodded, and Uncle James shrugged again. "We're okay. Just having a little heart to heart," he said. He stood and took the bag with the special cleaner from Mama.

"Gina, are you sure you're alright?" Mama pulled me aside while Uncle James and Ben cleaned the couch.

I rubbed my eyes. "I just miss home." I tried so hard to be strong, but my voice cracked. Mama's eyes softened and she gave me a hug.

"It's finally setting in, huh. It's strange for me too, I promise. We'll be okay though. This is how life is. Things change."

"That's what Uncle James said," I muttered. I helped Mama scoop the ice cream out into bowls, giving myself just a little bit extra. I deserved it.

"We'll talk more about what's going to happen later if

16

you want, okay?"

I just nodded. I took my bowl and a spoon and sighed a great big sigh. This was exhausting. There were so many people, so many adults in this one tiny space. I didn't have anywhere to be by myself! I loved Mama and Uncle James and Ben was okay but they just didn't get it.

"I am going to my drawing desk. Do not disturb me." Dramatically I turned and walked off. I went into me and Mama's shared room and sat at the desk. Pebbles, who had been locked up in the room, came and sat on my lap. She trilled at me.

"I'm sorry you've been locked up here," I crooned at her. She lifted her head up towards me, relishing in the pets and scritches. "It's not fair, no. But it's okay. Because I'm here now."

She mewed and purred, and I put a spoonful of ice cream into my mouth. I know it was strange and didn't make much sense, but I really felt so much better after crying. It all just came out, and now there was room for the happy, inspired feelings to live in my heart.

I hadn't drawn all week, since Mama and I had left Florida. I hadn't done anything that made me really happy since we had left, now that I thought about it. I opened my pencil case and pulled out my #2 pencils. My favorite one, the black Ticonderoga one. Those always had the best erasers. I looked down at Pebbles, the source of all of our chaos for the day, and back at the blank notebook paper in front of me.

I thought about the last time we'd sat like that back home. It had to have been not that long ago. We were in the living room. Mama was sorting soaps and oils for her shop. The windows were open, and the birds were chirping outside. Waves crashed on the beach in the distance. Our house plants were dancing in the soft salty breeze. Pebbles sat on my lap while I practiced my shading, a YouTube video in the background. The lady on the screen was showing me - her camera - the way she held her pencil, and how to apply pressure. I drew a circle with her and started practicing. The first one looked just like a stripey, blobby circle. It was frustrating, but I remember being determined.

"I should draw our home," I said out loud to Pebbles. She looked up at me with her big yellow eyes. She didn't know what I was saying, not the words, but I liked to think she understood anyway. She yawned and put her head on her paws, ready to watch the lines and shapes appear from my pencil onto the paper.

"Do you understand how this works little Pebbles?" I asked her, reaching over her to begin drawing.

I started with the background. That's what the lady on YouTube had said. There was background and middle ground and foreground. I said them out loud to myself as I drew.

In the background there were the other buildings and the smaller trees that made up the skyline. Middle ground was our house with its flat roof and garage and arched windows. The foreground was our driveway, the tree that grew front and center, and the bush of rosemary we thought would be fun to have but grew out of control that one summer. The image of the tree bending and the dark sky came into my head, but I pushed it aside, replacing it with the bright and sunny image I was trying to replicate.

"Where should I draw you?" I asked Pebbles once I was satisfied with the sketch. It was a light drawing, just an outline. My artistic process, Mama had called it once. It was true. Every artist had to have a process. Mine was like this.

Pebbles thought for a moment, then reached her paw out and tapped a corner of the page.

"By the driveway, that's a good choice." I pet her between her ears and went back to work drawing her fluffy figure in between the lines that would become the driveway.

Mama came in at some point to check on me.

"How are you girls doing here?" She picked up my now empty bowl of ice cream. "Pebbles can now be freed from her captivity."

I barely looked up. Pebbles just stretched. "It's okay," I said, putting the pencil between my teeth while I looked at my drawing. "She's sitting here. We're drawing."

"I see. Is that our house?" Mama put a hand on my shoulder as she looked over it at the sketch.

"Yes. When it was pretty and yellow and sunny. Not dark and grey."

"It looks just like it. Oh! Don't forget my rooster!" She laughed and pointed at the walkway leading from the driveway to the front door. She had had a rooster statue there before. It was hideous, I thought. But Mama loved it for some reason. She loved chickens. Not actually having them, but the look of them. She said they were like feathery dinosaurs. In my head, they were no different than other birds. But I loved the way Mama loved them, so I didn't mind it much.

"But I hated the rooster!"

I did. The chickens were fine, but the rooster? That was a different story. Roosters were just uglier than chickens. And at least the chickens were nice. Roosters were meanies. Probably.

"But it was an authentic part of our house!" Mama exclaimed back.

I laughed and shook my head. "I guess I'll add the

20

rooster."

Mama smiled. "I knew I could convince you. It looks really good!"

"Thank you!"

She took my bowl to the kitchen and I kept drawing.

An hour felt like no time at all, but by the end of it, I felt satisfied. The yellow house and green lawn and rosemary bush. Grey driveway, blue skies. The colorful picture looked just like everything I'd remembered. It looked like it did in the past. Like it had on all my walks home.

Pebbles jumped onto the desk and sniffed the paper.

"Do you approve?" I asked her, and she pawed at it. I took that as a yes.

Mama and Uncle James and Ben all really liked the drawing too. They gushed over it and hung it up on Uncle James' fridge. We sat and laughed, and for the first time since leaving our home, I thought this might not be so bad after all. I might just make it here.

It had taken some time, but I was starting to see the appeal of living here. Uncle James and I went to get groceries together every week while Mama looked for jobs. The cars buzzing by were something I would have to get used to, but people were really nice here!

21

The grocery store was very close by, so even though Uncle James and I drove there, it didn't take as long. And people really didn't care about how they dressed - but also cared a lot! I saw people in all sorts of outfits, and they didn't seem to care what other people thought about how they dressed. If anything, they defended their own clothes and styles so fast! There were goth girls and e boys and pretty people in floofy dresses. There was even this man Uncle James and I walked by every week who looked like he was out of an old timey disco. It was so cool!

That was a new thing I was learning. All the people were so different, but they all loved themselves. Or maybe they didn't, but were very good at faking it. Rachel used to say that - fake it till you make it. She said that's what she had done to make all those friends. It didn't seem right to me when she did it, but it didn't seem wrong to think about all of these people doing just that. It's like nobody cared about what anybody else did.

I still wasn't prepared for how boring it would be though, sitting in an apartment. I couldn't just go out like I used to. Mama said it was too dangerous, and Uncle James said I would definitely get lost. What was I supposed to do now? I had gone through half of my notebook already with drawings and doodles and sketches. One day, I even got the idea to use Pebble's paws to make something. She...wasn't so happy about it. But it looked great!

"Pleeeeaaase can we please just go somewhere?" I begged Mama and Uncle James. It was late August at this point, and we'd been here for a month now. Mama had been job searching, with no luck, and Uncle James had been working. A lot. But that meant we never did anything. What was the point of all of this if we didn't do anything? We went to the park all the time, but it was just a park and I didn't even have any friends.

"Alright, alright, where do you want to go?" Mama asked. She brought down her laptop screen to look at me.

I thought hard for a moment. "Can we go to the zoo? Or the aquarium? Uncle James said that the biggest aquarium in the country is here!"

"Maybe, but we should wait for them to open their dolphin exhibit again," he replied, clicking his pen a couple times.

"But the zoo?"

"Okay, yeah, we'll go to the zoo." Mama conceded.

I knew that it was a big ask, because of how busy she and Uncle James had been, but this was so exciting! We were finally going to go somewhere!

"YAAAYYY!" I jumped up and hugged her and then hugged Uncle James. "FINALLY!"

They laughed and hugged me back. It was starting to feel more normal, living here, being here. It really wasn't so bad.

BATH BOMBS

“I told you, it's not that big of a deal. I don't know why you're worrying so much. You and Gina just got here. She's had a hard enough time as it is.”

"Don't talk to me like I don't know about my daughter, James. I just don't want to impose any longer than we have."

"You haven't, at no point did I say that you had!"

It was late at night. I was supposed to be asleep. School was going to start soon, so Mama was having me prepare to get up early. School started way earlier around here. But I couldn't sleep, so I was up, and that's when I heard the whisper-yelling in the living room. I peered through the crack in the door and listened in.

It wasn't news to me that Mama was getting fed up here. We'd been so used to being on our own, in our own place. I didn't know that much about Mama and Uncle James' growing up, but they were always so close. But maybe there was stuff I didn't know about. They never talked about grown up stuff with me. But Mama had been searching for a job for around two months now, and we were getting close to school starting, and it wasn't hard for me to connect the dots.

A couple weeks ago was when we had gotten the call that our house back in Florida was gone for good. And Mama's shop. And my school. It was all gone. And for some reason, I just wasn't as sad as I thought I would be. I think I had just known, from that day months ago when we were loading into our car and running away from the coming storm, that would be the last time I'd see it. I had hoped and dreamed about going back, but in the back of my mind, I think I just knew. So it wasn't as sad when the news broke.

But now, we didn't know what we would do. And that's what the whisper-yells coming from the living room were about. I didn't mean to, but I leaned a little too hard on the door and spilled out onto the floor.

Mama and Uncle James both turned and looked at me, both suddenly bashful.

"Sorry, Gina, we didn't mean to wake you!"

"Everything's okay!"

They stumbled over each other's words in their apologies. I just shook my head and rubbed my eyes. The lights were brighter in the living room than in the bedroom. Pebbles came out around me, yawning and jumping up onto the couch. The fall had woken her up too, and she had decided to choose the spot in the middle of everyone to snuggle up.

"I was awake," I stood and walked to sit next to Pebbles. "Why are you guys fighting?"

Mama sighed. She came and sat beside me. "We weren't fighting. Just...a heated discussion."

"That's the same thing." I shook my head. "About what?"

Mama and Uncle James looked at each other. Uncle James sat down too, next to Mama.

"Okay, you know we've been here for a few months now, and things back home aren't as good as we thought?"

I nodded.

Mama continued, "Well...I've been trying to find a job, somewhere around here like what I had back in Florida. I don't know if there are any small stores like that hiring. So...I thought about starting my own. Just like I did before."

"Okay, so what does that have to do with living here?"

"Your mom wants to be able to move out. Both of you out. I know that's what you both want, ultimately. I just...I don't know if it's the right time. Especially since she's just started the process of starting her new business. I know, it's a lot of grown up stuff and we'll figure it out between the two of us. Finding somewhere stable for you and Pebbles. And getting you guys your own place. Don't you worry about it."

I thought about everything they said and hugged Pebbles close.

"I don't understand any of it," I finally admitted. "I don't get what the big deal is. Mama you did it all once before. And we're okay here."

"I know we're okay I just-" She huffed, frustrated. "I want to give you what we had before. That's all."

"And you'll do that," Uncle James said. "You'll get it all back, as much as you can. It's just going to take some time, you know that." He looked at me. "Gina, I'm so sorry we woke you. But don't worry about it. Your mother's headstrong, you know it, I know it."

He teased her, lightening the mood. Mama rolled her eyes, but couldn't help but smile a little bit. "Says you," she shot back at him. Then she turned to me once more. "We'll be okay. We just might have some difficult times for a little bit, that's all."

"It can't be more difficult than leaving." I hadn't thought before the words slipped out of my mouth. It's not that it was a painful statement, but a very matter of fact one. I thought it was true. The most difficult thing I'd ever had to do was leave. And I did it. Mama did it with me. Even Pebbles did it. And we were all doing our best with it. Even though we all got grouchy sometimes.

A moment passed and Uncle James shook his head. "You kids are so perceptive, nothing gets past you."

Mama smiled and took my hand. "No, you're right. The hard part is over. Out with the old, in with the new. I'm so sorry, I didn't mean to involve you in this."

I just squeezed her hand. "It's okay."

"Okay, it's very late. Let's sleep, shall we? Still need to get prepared for school!" Mama squeezed my hand back, then let it go to stand.

I groaned. "I don't know why I have to go to school after

all of this," I whined.

"Because that's what kids do! Come on!"

Mama helped me up and nudged me towards our room. I laid in my bed, wondering what would happen next, what the new school would be like, if I'd meet another Rachel or someone else to be my best friend. Eventually, I closed my eyes and they stayed closed, and I slept.

The first day of school crept up on me faster than I would have liked. It was like only yesterday, I'd been with my old friends back in Florida, hanging out together. We would braid each other's hair and dance and gossip and eat s'mores.

I panicked every time I thought about whether or not I'd be able to get that here too. Would the kids be nice to me?? It was the sixth grade. They'd probably all known each other for a long time! I had never been the weird new kid before.

"You'll be fine," Mama said as she was brushing my hair. We were going to go to the mall and get some new clothes for school. I hadn't said anything, but I was biting my nails, and Mama knew. She said everyone always had a tell for when they were nervous or scared. Mine was nail biting.

"What if I don't make friends?" I bit on my pinkie nail.

She swatted my hand. "Don't do that or you won't have anything left. And you'll make friends, Gina. You're a very smart, capable young lady. You're kind and caring. You'll get to meet lots of new people. You'll find the ones that you like and that like you. Simple."

"I wish we could have moved to New York with Rachel and her parents. Then we could all be together." I pouted.

"Honey, Rachel's grandparents live in New York. That's why they went there. Uncle James lives here in Georgia, so that's why we're here. I know you miss your friends, but sometimes things just happen. You still talk to Rachel, it's not like she's not your friend anymore."

And she was right, I did still talk to Rachel on Zoom every couple weeks. But it wasn't the same. She hadn't been the same since she had moved either. She was already different from me, but now she used different words and was kind of mean. She said there was so much I just "didn't get" the last time we talked. She had a new boyfriend in New York already. I was happy for her, I was. But maybe Mama was wrong about Rachel not being my friend still.

I let out a big long breath. "She's not not my friend, but it's not like she's my friend the same way." The words could have made more sense, but she knew what I meant. "I just want to be included. I don't like being weird."

Mama tied off my hair and put her hands on my shoulders. "Being weird is good. It means you're different. It means you're yourself. You don't have to reflect everyone around you to be valuable. Believe me."

She kissed the top of my head and walked away to put the brush in the drawer. "I was the weird one in school when I was your age."

"And?" I looked up at her.

"And...I think I'm doing alright now." She sat next to me on the bed. "Look, you haven't even started at your new school yet. You don't know what wonderful people are there. Don't discount their ability to like you, or your ability to fit in, before you've even gotten a chance."

I nodded. "I wish I could take Pebbles with me. She could just sit in my backpack. She's like a stuffed animal anyways. My emotional support animal." I scooped her up in my arms and cradled her like a baby.

"I wish you could too. But you know she'd escape the minute you opened your book bag. Imagine her, running through the hallways of your new school! Now that...that would be weird." Mama teased me, petting Pebbles' furry belly before she squirmed out of my arms.

I scrunched up my nose and stuck my tongue out at Pebbles. "Well, fine be like that." She just scurried away before I could pick her up again.

It was honestly shocking how lucky Mama had gotten with starting up her business again. She told me she worked really hard, and anyone could see that, but there was no way she found a place so close to Uncle James' that had everything she needed to open a shop. It was a coincidence that the rug store a few miles down had gone out of business. Sad for them, but great for us. In the weeks before school started, I was now helping Mama sweep the floors, clean the walls, paint them, and start picking out all of the new decorations and even some of the inventory for the kids sections.

I always thought Mama's business was cool. She sold soaps in bars and in little pump jars, dried flowers, salts, oils, and sometimes even shirts and aprons and containers for all the salts and flowers and oils. Sometimes she sold makeup. Before we moved, she had been trying to get into something she called having a "green store." Things like refillable soaps and shampoos and stuff. For the environment. It was funny since her old store was destroyed by a storm.

"Gina, what do you think about these sponge loofahs? Are they cool? They're all small and handheld so kids can use them. Is it good for that section?"

Mama handed me the iPad. On the screen, there were pictures of small sponges the size of my hand. I squinted and furrowed my eyebrows.

"I don't know if that's what kids want..." I handed it back to her. "I don't know, kids like fun things. Like bubbles and colorful things that fizz and stuff. You're a mom, you're supposed to know."

"Yeah, but you're a kid so you know even better than I do!" She countered back with a smile. She swiped a few more times.

"Okay, what about something like this then? Bath bombs! This creator makes them with little toys inside. I don't think I can sell those for kids though. They did ban those chocolate eggs...do they need to be plain?"

"I don't think anyone is going to eat their bath bombs, Mama." I tied off the end of a paper flower I had spent the last ten minutes unfolding and poofing open and handed it to her.

Mama took the last paper flower from me and hung it from the ceiling. The hardest part was done. We'd finally set up the shop and we were ready to stock! It was such an exciting moment as we both stood back and admired our progress.

The walls were all an ivory white with black curvy stripes running along them like old timey mod living rooms would have had. Except instead of being ugly and orange and brown like they had been in our inspiration pictures on Pinterest, these were simple black. They created a balance in the room, so the racks stood out.

The rug shop that had been here previously had the prettiest chandeliers hanging on the front and back of the shop too. The first one had brass lines coming out from a center point, each end fixed with a flower-shaped light fixture. It was like a flower made out of a flower! The one in the back was more traditional, with crystal parts and shiny bits. They were both pretty. Mama said they made the place look "lux." It was that for sure. We had added our paper flowers to tie it all together so they'd be up and ready for opening day.

"We did it, Gina." Mama hugged me tight. "We did it. Look at this place. Look how far we've come!"

"Are we moving out of Uncle James' place soon then?" I looked up at her.

Truth was, we'd been with Uncle James for as long

as either of them was comfortable with. It had been two months, Mama had a job, I was starting school. We needed our own place.

"Not quite yet. Once we start making a net profit. That means making money." She wiped her hands on her coveralls. "That should be soon though."

"It's a little bit like things being normal again." I took some steps back and held my hands up like a frame for the scene before me. "I can help you with the shop, and we'll have our own place with Pebbles." It was just almost normal now. Almost.

FUNNEL CAKE

For the first time in two months, everything felt good again. Mama's business was up and running. We even had a ribbon cutting and everything! It was so much fun, and now there was something for us to all do, at least until school started.

"So when are we going to get our own place?" I asked Mama while helping her unload the boxes of goodies for the day. The bestsellers were the soaps and face creams, so we seemed to get more of those every week.

"Hopefully soon!" Mama replied. She began stacking the soaps from the boxes into a cart to take into the store. "You know, it's been a very crazy few months but we really pulled it together. I know you've been missing your friends and home and the transition has been hard, but I'm really proud of you."

"I know." I took the scissors carefully and started to cut at the tape along the center of the box. "Leaving was hard but it's not like anyone was waiting for us back there. I mean, even Rachel moved on."

"I know that sucks, but it happens. You know, I had a best friend when I was your age that moved away too. She and her family moved to Colorado...oh, I don't know, twenty years ago? We'd been friends for years. When she came back for Thanksgiving, I barely recognized her. But that doesn't mean you're not friends at all or you won't ever be friends again in the same way."

Mama took the broken down boxes and stacked them

to the side by our recycling pile.

I didn't say anything. It had been hard, seeing my best friend change so much. I knew we were both becoming different people, but it was hard to accept that we would have to be different like this. And there was nothing wrong with it, it just wasn't right for me.

That's what I had realized the last time Mama and I spoke about it. I had never thought about being friends with someone or having to work on being friends with someone. She told me that's what happens when you grow up, but that when you work for friends they mean more. She also said I spent too much time around adults that summer too, so maybe going back to school would help me see that I wasn't actually as awkward as I felt now. I hoped she was right.

We walked around into the front of the store to restock. A woman and a young girl walked in just then to browse. I tucked myself around the lotions corner, not wanting to interact with customers. It was always awkward explaining that no, I wasn't a ten year old that worked in a store and yes, I was just helping, and yes I could stop if I wanted to. People were very nosy, I had learned.

"Moooom, please can we get this? It smells so good and I can wear it to school! It's not even that bright, it's just a little pink."

The girl showed her mom the tube of tinted lip balm.

"I don't know, Olivia, you're a little young to be wearing

makeup." The woman turned over a bar of soap to read the ingredients.

"But it's not makeup, it's just chapstick. See!" Olivia showed her mom the tube, and her mom shrugged.

"Huh, I guess you're right. Okay, but just the one." She put Olivia's tube in her basket and kept shopping.

The girl turned and spotted me, and waved. She had brown curly hair that bounced around her face and kind eyes. She was wearing a purple cheetah print shirt and blue jeans and had all sorts of pins stuck to her back pack.

I waved back at her, a little embarrassed to have been caught.

"Hi! I'm Olivia!" She came up to me and held out her hand while her mother checked out. Both of our moms glanced at the two of us and smiled at each other.

I looked at Mama, then at her, and took her hand, giving it a firm shake. "I'm Gina."

"Nice to meet you Gina! I haven't seen you before, do you go to Westside?"

"Yeah, I do. We just moved here..." I trailed off, not sure what to do now.

Olivia didn't seem to notice or care. "Oh that's cool! We've been here forever! Where did you move from?"

I was a little taken aback by her friendliness and up-front-ness, but I found myself smiling. "Oh, um, Florida. Just a couple months ago."

Olivia's eyes widened at those words. "Oh my god, like because of the storm? I'm so sorry! We saw that on the news it looked scary! But like, you're here now! We're going to be friends."

She finished off her statement with a grin, and hugged me. The air left my mouth and I laughed a little to play it off, hugging her back.

"Okay, Olivia, come on. It was nice to meet you and your mom, Gina!" Olivia's mom came and got her, having given us a couple moments even after checking out to talk. I guess her and Mama chatted too.

"Nice to meet you too!" I said, and they were gone as soon as they'd come. I couldn't totally make sense of what had happened, but it felt good!

Mama looked at me. "See! I told you you would make friends! She seems like such a lovely young lady."

"She was nice. That wasn't too weird either!"

She laughed. "I told you! You're not weird! You're just out of practice. Looks like you're going to have a friend going into school. Her mom and I exchanged numbers so you both can hang out."

"Do you think we'll see them again?" I bit my nails and apprehensively thought about what was to come now that I had actually started talking to a new friend.

"Probably. I'd like to meet her mom more before you two spend time together, but I'm sure that can be arranged. And they'll surely be back in the store." Mama went back behind her counter and looked at her clipboard.

I wasn't sure why, but I was beginning to get nervous again at the thought of being back to school. It was paired with the same amount of excitement to see Olivia again and possibly hang out and do friend things again like sleepovers and maybe go to the mall together.

But how did I even know that would happen? What if she said mean things about me behind my back to all her friends and actually they would hate me when school started? It was beginning to stress me out. She seemed cool, but I couldn't tell anymore. I thought Rachel was cool, but even she started being mean to me.

"Don't overthink it," I heard Mama say. I turned around.

"Huh?"

"You're chewing your nails again, you're overthinking it. It'll happen if it's meant to happen. You have so much to offer in friendships, you know that. I know that. James knows that. Pebbles especially knows that. Just enjoy that you go to meet someone nice for now."

She put her clipboard down and leaned forward against the counter.

I sat up on the step ladder propped up against one of the walls. "I'm not trying to. I just want everything to be okay and make new friends and not get made fun of."

"And what would she make fun of you for?" Mama

asked with a raised eyebrow.

I shrugged. "I'm not sure, but she'd find something! People always find something."

"You're right, they do. So why give them any more power?"

That got me thinking a little more. Mama was right. I was giving them power by believing them. I didn't get anything out of being sad. All that happened was I got sad. And being sad didn't help me make friends or feel okay about making friends.

"You're right..." I begrudged.

"I often times am right." Mama came around and gave my shoulders a squeeze. "Your nerves will be calmed soon enough, I'm sure. You start back next week. Should we go shopping sometime soon?"

I shrugged and held her arm around me. "I think so. I think I have enough clothes now. I should probably get a backpack and some pens...Can I get a new sketchbook?"

"Only if you promise not to draw in class." Mama held out her pinky finger.

I looped mine around her. "Pinky promise."

Uncle James had left a flier on the kitchen counter for us. It was for a hot air balloon competition! And you could go and ride them! There were supposed to be hundreds of them.

The only problem was I was scared of heights. After everything I had been through, it seemed like something that small wouldn't bother me, but it did! I felt like I was falling all the time, even if I wasn't. I couldn't even go to the jungle gyms when I was little because of it. It was so bad. And so the panic came over me again looking at the flier. But it looked like so much fun.

I couldn't figure out what it was I wanted. Of course I wanted to go, Uncle James and Mama would both be there, and they were fun. Maybe I could make more friends? Maybe Olivia would be there? There were so many good reasons to go, but I couldn't see them clearly. I thought about what it felt like to be high up, looking down at the world below. Even the thought of it made my heart beat faster and my breath became shallower for a moment.

I put the flier down and sat on the couch. Pebbles came and sat next to me, reaching her paws out to ask for pets. I began petting her, and listened to Mama talk about how this was such a good idea for us.

"We should start going to things like this!" She started rummaging through the cabinets for a pot to make dinner.

"Will we have to go into one of them?" I asked her. Pebbles was now in my lap. She was purring and rubbing her head against my hands and my chin.

"I don't think you'd have to if you didn't want to," Mama said. She had gotten out the cutting board and some onions. "I'm thinking about making pasta, does that sound good?"

I nodded. "Yes, that sounds good. I bet the balloons would be pretty. I don't want to go in one though. That sounds really scary."

"You know, if they actually have a ton, they might not let people in. Hey, maybe there will be carnival food! When was the last time we got funnel cake?"

Mama smiled at me from across the room and started cooking. The air smelled like onions and garlic and basil, and I could hear the oil simmering. It filled the whole room like the most delicious cloud.

"Ooooh funnel cake!" The nerves and fear of being high up began to fade upon realizing I may not have to do that. We could just watch from far away and see them all! And funnel cake sounded really good. "I think I was seven or something right?"

"I think so, yeah. It's been a long time. It'll be good for us to go out and get treats and all that. Maybe if it happens every year, we can make it our little thing."

"I'd like that! Can we ask Olivia to come with us? And her mom too of course." I perked up and held Pebbles close so she didn't fall. She didn't like that though, and wiggled out of my hands. She sat next to me, licking her fur to set it back in the right place.

"I can text her and ask, yeah."

Then Mama poured a can of tomatoes into the mix and the sizzling sound completely changed. I could smell the sauce start to cook down and perfume everything around us. It reminded me of being back home, and working on homework at the dining table while Mama cooked.

"Thank you!" I jumped up and walked over to the kitchen island to peer at what she was doing. "I'm very hungry now."

"I bet you are! You get the plates. It's almost done." Mama stirred her pot and I set the table.

The hot air balloon festival was here! I was so excited to go! I put on my new jeans and new shirt and favorite sneakers. It was my first weekend after school started and I was so ready to do something before all my time got filled up with school and after school classes and homework.

When we got there, we immediately saw them. The hot air balloons. They were huge, floating like big orbs. It was shocking that they weren't bouncing against each other with how close they were.

"Gina hiiiiii!"

I heard my name called from behind me and turned. Oliva was running towards me full speed with her arms out. I held mine out just in time for her to crash into me. We both fell over and laughed.

"Oh my god, I'm so glad you're here! My mom told me that y'all were planning on coming. I'm so glad you did! It's so pretty we've been coming since I was a baby! Come on, we've got to go get food!" She took my arm and excitedly pulled me along with her towards the food stations.

The atmosphere was so lively. There were people playing instruments, dancing, and laughing. The smell of funnel cake and snow cones and Dole whips seemed to guide us to the stands. There were food trucks lined up from all different restaurants and types of foods. There were gyros and Mexican and noodles and pizza and burgers! So much was happening! I was glad we came.

We all got our food. Olivia and I got funnel cakes and pizza. Mama got gyros and a snow cone. Uncle James got a funnel cake too and a snow cone. We pushed through the crowds and found a nice spot to lay out our blankets and watch the balloons bob up and down.

"They're so pretty!" I exclaimed, staring up at them. This was the best. My face was sticky with powdered sugar, which somehow made the pizza even better. We had water and slushies to wash down all the food. The air was hot, but not as sticky as it sometimes was. The grass was soft. The balloons looked so peaceful against all the buzzing below.

Olivia broke off a piece of her funnel cake and nodded as she ate it. "They're very pretty. Sometimes they let you go up in one if you're lucky. I've never done it or seen it, but that's what they say. Aren't you so happy you came? This is the best. I love it. I can't wait to be older and go to more things."

"That sounds a little scary, going up in the balloons," I hesitated. "But I am glad we're here. It's really fun. We didn't do things like this in Florida. It didn't happen in our town."

"Are you scared of heights or something?" Olivia asked between bites and swigs of her slushie.

"Yeah. I always get scared of falling. What if I get hurt? That would be bad!" I shrugged and leaned back onto my hands. "You're not scared?"

She shook her head. "Not of heights. But I don't like swimming if my feet can't touch the ground." She shivered at the thought.

"Oh, I love swimming," I said. "That's the thing I miss the most. The beach and swimming in the ocean."

"You're so brave!" Olivia said with big eyes. "But I guess it's the same for me because I don't mind being high up. I went on a plane once and it was so cool!"

I shook my head. "See, I couldn't do that."

"I have an idea!" Olivia's eyes lit up and she sat straight as she explained. "You go in one of the hot air balloons with me, and I'll go swimming with you! We'll both do things we're scared of!"

I looked up at the sky, then back at her. Me? Go up on a hot air balloon? My heart began racing, but I then thought of the other half of her idea. She felt like I did about swimming, and she was willing to go. If I went up into a hot air balloon.

I took in a big deep breath, and slowly let it out. "Mama, can we go find someone giving hot air balloons?"

Olivia squealed. "YES!" She threw her arms around me. "We're going on a balloon ride!!!"

Mama looked at me with a mixture of shock and pride. "Yeah, we can find someone. Are you sure?"

I nodded. "I'm sure."

And so we walked around, trying to find someone to give us a ride. Every time I felt my fear rise up again, I took a few breaths and let it go. I would be okay. I would be with Mama. And Olivia. It would be okay.

After a little while we found someone with their balloon on the ground, and we got in. As we started going up, I focused on Olivia and her excitement to bring down my own fears.

Eventually, we were up in the air and stopped. I could see the balloons around me, and peering down over the edge, it all seemed so small. Mama held my hand as reassurance. I wouldn't fall.

Uncle James was the size of an ant from this far up. And the balloons that had looked so small from below, were huge from up here. It was beautiful.

I realized then how much I had changed in the past two months. I had become an entirely new person. I was stronger. Braver. And who knew where I would go from there.

Everything could only go up.